Crime For the Holidays

BONNIE ELIZABETH

MY BIG FAT ORANGE CAT PUBLISHING

Contents

Introduction

It seems like the holidays should be a great time for something nice and cozy and sweet and yet none of these stories are sweet. Given my penchant for writing cozy mysteries, you'd think that there would be some level of sweetness. But in virtually all of these mysteries there is something very rotten at the heart and often in the main character. Even my cozy sleuth is rather full of herself and every bit as annoying and self-important as some of the early British detectives.

We start with A Crafty Affair, which is set at a holiday craft fair. It opens the tale because it's the coziest of the stories and because a craft fair is a great way to begin the holidays.

The Leftovers Club is set the Sunday after Thanksgiving and is about a group of women who are alone during the holidays. They get together to chat and support each other through the holidays. But at least one of them has a secret they're keeping from the others.

The season moves right along with The Advent Calendar Deaths which pits a mob fixer against a disgruntled husband. It takes place sometime during advent though well before Christmas.

The Best Christmas Ever starts at a company holiday party early in December and ends at a family party closer to Christmas eve. It'd be a frivolous account of company parties and intrigues if there wasn't an unexpected death.

Finally, as we near the holiday, we meet a lonely acupuncturist in *An Unexpectedly Nice Christmas.* Of course, with the crime that starts her holiday and the people she celebrates it with, it's not exactly what she was hoping for, but then again, it was either that or spend it all alone.

Cuddle up for your reading and enjoy your hot cocoa or perhaps a hot buttered run and give thanks that your holidays are calmer than the ones in this volume.

A Crafty Affair

A Crafty Affair was first published as part of Kristine Kathryn Rusch's First Holiday Spectacular. It starts off this volume because it happens so soon after Thanksgiving. It's also the lightest of the crimes and like good wine, a lighter mystery should always be enjoyed before moving on to the more full-bodied ones. The narrator is annoying but the setting is fun and familiar to anyone who has done some of their holiday shopping at a local craft fair. And the crime, well, our nosey narrator is more than happy to tell you all about it.

I wondered what the young man was doing, fondling the yarn over at Rita's table. She always has these large rolled balls of yarn in holiday colors sitting in dishes, probably because the blankets she crochets need to be hung on quilt racks rather than folded on the tables and her booth would look lopsided and funny without something on the table itself.

She sells a few potholders, but most people go for mine because Rita sells hers for far too much money. She says she has to pay for her time as well as her yarn. I figure crocheting is something I'd do anyway and selling it covers the cost of my hobby and a little more, so I'm happy. Rita, however, seems to find that money makes her happy, but, to each her own, I guess.

The Arden Holiday Festival—there was quite an outcry over that naming, believe me—is when I make most of my craft money. Like Rita, I crochet. While I'm fond enough of Rita, I sort of wished our tables weren't right across the aisle. Of course, I don't make many blankets, preferring to make hats and scarves and shawls—although shawls don't sell like they used to, so now I'm making tree skirts, which do. By eleven, when the young looking man was oddly intent upon the ball of yarn and stuffing something inside, I'd sold seven scarves, four hats, two sets of mittens, and six tree skirts, including an ugly red ombre design. No accounting for taste, I suppose.

I'd listened to a dozen women shopping ooh and ahh over my stuff, two complain about Rita's prices, and several discuss the hit and run out on Old Black Mill Road. Penny Whitesmith had been killed out there, walking home from her workplace in downtown Arden, at the Arden Building, which held the Holiday Festival. In fact, with Penny's demise there had been talk of cancelling, but other city workers stepped up and made sure we were not without our festival.

The Arden Building is a sprawling old thing. They'd tried to make it a mall to revitalize downtown, but that effort had failed miserably. Now they rented out smaller spaces to local businesses. There's still a huge walkway in the middle where the place is covered, like a mall. There's a coffee shop, which was open today, and the smell of fresh brew was so strong I didn't even need to drink a cup to wake up.

Long tables with bright cloths covering them were placed in two rows on either side of the walkway. Some people brought their own backdrops, but others, like me, were content to sit in front of a closed shop. Fortunately, I was in front of an accountant who had a tasteful set of brown blinds in the narrow window that looked out to the central area.

Marci, who makes soaps was on my left. Rita was across the way. There was a jewelry maker next to her. There was a small aisle between me and Rodney who makes metal wind chimes out of old spoons and forks and such. He never sells much but he's there every year, just like I am.

Across from him was a new young woman selling all sorts of cat jewelry. While I'm more of a horse person—after all I do live in Central Kentucky—I was quite taken with the stuff and was considering getting a pair of earrings. I love earrings. My husband says I love earrings almost as much as I love to be nosey. I've always told him that without me, he'd never know what was happening in Arden.

Whit Nelson came by in his police uniform, set to keep an eye on things. Not that there's ever a real need. The shoplifters go elsewhere. No one wants to try and lift crafts from a bunch of folks who just made it, at least not in Arden. They particularly do not do things like that around my booth. Everyone knows I have an eagle eye.

"How you doing, Miz Gayle?" he asked.

"Doing great," I said. "A little slow. Last year I'd sold more scarves by this time."

In fact, last year, by just after lunch, I'd sold so much, I was putting out my potholders, which I only make the last week, just in case I sell out of everything else. Last year had been particularly good, but this year was a bit slower than average, though still not too bad. I noticed Rita hadn't sold a thing.

"Ben's setting up the bourbon table outside for tasting," Whit said, smiling and nodding.

Ben ran a bar that sold an assortment of bourbon and it was the place to go for bourbon tasting—if you had to stay in Arden, which most people don't. I just nodded at Whit and he moved on, talking to Marci. There weren't too many people around just then so I slipped out of my booth and hurried over to Rita's. She was talking to a young woman with a toddler on her hip about one of the afghans. It was a large lap blanket in multiple colors with a pattern the look of a knitted fisherman's pattern, all knotted and bumpy.

I looked over the yarn and started pushing my fingers into the green ombre ball of yarn and felt something small and cool and hard. I grabbed it and was about to turn when Rita looked at me and nodded.

"What can I get you, Gayle?" she asked.

"I was just admiring that same afghan," I said pointing to the one the woman was fingering. It was pale peach, cream, and a deep rust brown in stripes. I wasn't keen on the stripes. I think it would have looked better in plain cream but I'm a traditionalist about my patterns.

Rita beamed as if she'd won the lottery. "Really?"

I nodded, smiling tightly. I was looking at it. I found it interesting. It wasn't a pattern I was familiar with. I didn't actually want to be familiar with that pattern.

Rita then went on to tell me about the work and the pattern and what gave her the idea. The woman who had been admiring it wandered off. I wasn't too surprised. A girl her age carrying a toddler probably couldn't afford almost two hundred dollars for a glorified lap blanket.

Two older women who looked familiar from other years paused at my booth, and I hurried back to chat with them. The chat resulted in a sale of four more scarves, two hats, a pair of mittens, and a white and silver tree skirt. I carefully marked all of that down as I took in their money. They paid with a credit card and I used my cell phone to run it through Square.

My grandson, Tyler, who's in sixth grade and was going to be singing carols later on with his class, had told me about taking credit cards online. He and his mother helped me set up Square on my cellphone the year before, and I think that's one of the reasons I'd had such a good year.

After bagging up the assorted products as directed by the women, I was able to settle down and examine what I had in my hand. It was a small card about the size of my thumb and very flat. I hadn't noticed anything like that before so I got out my cell phone to call Tyler. He may be young but he knows technical stuff.

Fortunately, he agreed to come by before they stated playing Santa Claus is Coming to Town far too loudly. I've noticed that the spiritual carols tended to be played more softly than the silly ones. I think they all should have been played more softly, except for Joy to the World which almost demands to be played at full volume.

While waiting for Tyler, I sold another scarf. I chatted with Mark, a short little man who sells pumpkins at the farmer's market in the late summer and early fall. He also sells an amazing yellow watermelon in August. Mark moved on to chat with Marci about her soaps. He even purchased some, probably for his wife. I couldn't imagine him going out smelling like pumpkin spice or chai latte, which were Marci's top scents this year. Of course, I couldn't imagine going out smelling like that as a woman either. Who would want to unless you worked at a grocery store or maybe a coffee shop?

Tyler wandered over. He's still a bit of a towhead. I remember his mother at that age and her hair was already starting to turn mousy, like mine. I'm not sure where he gets the lighter coloring as his father is darker haired and dark eyed.

Tyler has brown eyes to go with that blonde hair. I don't envy my daughter when girls start noticing him. So many women my age tell me that it's good he's a boy, but really, boys are just as culpable and in many ways, in today's world, they have to be more so. Not that I think that's a bad thing. It's just been a long time coming, and we have society to challenge when bringing him up to be respectful, not just of authority, which is hard enough, but of girls in general. My daughter Denise agonizes over those questions often when we meet for lunch, which I try to make sure we do at least once a month.

Family is important, and I don't care what sort of family it is. My son has a husband and they live in Maryland because it's easier there, or so he says. I hate that he has to be that far away, but I want him to be happy. When he returns with his husband at Christmas, I hear about it from the women at church, which is why I so rarely go any longer.

"What's up, Grandma?" Tyler asked, coming around the table to join me inside the booth. Three young women walked by, one fingering the scarves. She looked up to see me watching and she blushed a bit and then turned away.

I hope I didn't look disapproving. My daughter says I have one of those faces.

"I found this." I handed the thing to Tyler. "I want to know what it is."

Tyler turned it over and read the name on it. San Disc 32 GB.

"It looks like a memory card for a camera like Mom got me last year," Tyler said. "Can I have it?"

"Do you have your camera with you?" I asked. He had a little camera, a pocket camera, but it had a few manual settings that allowed him to play with photographic effects before he sent the photos to Photoshop Elements, which he also had. Tyler is quite the little photographer in training. Of course, Denise always had a good eye, and I have several of her prints in my home.

Tyler nodded. He pulled it out of the pocket of his gray winter jacket. He was wearing it casually as children do, hanging off of him. His jeans were getting just a little short and I could see the edges of the tops of his high top sneakers. I thought we'd just gotten him new jeans before school started. He inserted the card into the camera and turned the thing on. The screen was small enough that I had to put on my reading glasses to look at the photos.

The first two were just of the city, the lights just coming on as the sun was setting. There were wreaths hanging from the downtown lamp posts and several of the buildings had their windows painted. Although I couldn't make out the details, I mentally filled them in.

Then we came to a photo of Old Black Mill Road. Penny was turning to wave at the photographer, smiling. The next one showed her turned back and walking along the edge. There was no sidewalk but less than half a mile up, one began again at the subdivision where she lived. Beside the road where she walked was a deep gulch so that no one could walk further off the side—this was a known issue and the people had often lobbied for a sidewalk to be put in there—and the trees that grew alongside the road, in the gulch, were pretty, just damp enough with cool water that they seemed to twinkle.

It had been a very wet year.

The next photo showed a car swerving towards Penny. I had heard there was a thick patch of ice just at the curve, which had probably caused the accident in the first place. If the driver hadn't left, no one would have put blame on them, but now, the tongues were wagging. Not mine, of course, except to correct inaccuracies that other people were spouting.

"Whoa!" Tyler said, clearly aware of what was happening. I tried to take the camera away, but he moved just out of reach and hit next.

Still looking over Tyler's shoulder, I saw a photo of the car stopped, and a man standing by the driver's side. It looked like the mayor. Not a man I'm fond of, mind you. He's a little too full of himself, but with his tall, lanky frame, and hair that he dyes a dark black—although he's only a few years younger than I am—he's hard to miss. Not to mention that long, ash gray duster he wears. Men in this part of Kentucky rarely dress like that.

The next photo showed a woman getting out of the car. Her face was turned towards the camera. It was Rita, dressed to the nines in black pumps and a dark dress under a gray wool coat that I knew was well made and quite warm.

Her mouth was open in a little donut, though something about her stance suggested she was less horrified than she might have been.

The earlier shots had had the sun just setting, so it couldn't have been too late. Penny wouldn't have been walking down the road that late at night. Whatever was happening, the mayor and Rita had to have been on their way to it. It was certainly possible the mayor had started drinking earlier and the patch of ice sealed the deal. It's well known he likes his bourbon.

The curve where Penny had been hit was well-lit and the camera captured the fact that the lights were working, although I'm certain the police had already ascertained that. The curve did tend to be shady with all the trees which meant it was a place that often didn't unfreeze even when the rest of the road did.

Old Black Mill Road was a back way up and over to Versailles and then into Lexington, which, given the dress, would have been my guess as to where the two were going. Except that Rita was married to Bill, who was most definitely not the mayor, and the mayor was married to Carole, who was not Rita. If I'm not mistaken, Carole had left to go visit her parents in Florida.

I'm sure the right person could have explained things, except the next picture showed Rita pulling the mayor away with a touch that looked intimate to me. Her head was cocked to one side, and she was looking up at him, her lips pressed out as if she were going to kiss him.

It was the final picture that took away any doubt that there was something more going on. A kiss that didn't look at all quick at the back of the car, obscuring the license plate, which I should have been looking at, but if needed I could flip the pictures back.

"Totally whoa," Tyler said.

"Give me the memory card," I said quietly.

"Why?" He loved this. It was a scandal and he was in the middle of it, ready to break it wide open. I expected the mayor had probably gotten a gift much like this one. No doubt someone wanted them to buy their silence.

Tyler flicked the next button again. Another photo, this one of the car lights going on and then a final one of the car driving off.

Penny had laid on the roadside half the night before someone finally noticed her lying just under the guardrail. I wondered if someone had pushed her over there, someone like the mayor, and that moment just wasn't captured on camera.

Unfortunately for Penny, she was dead before anyone spotted her.

"Tyler." I gave him my sternest voice. It had worked on Denise and her brother. I hoped it worked on Tyler.

Tyler moved around swinging his arms and shaking his head, his eyes rolling around like little marbles, but he pulled the card from his camera and gave it back. He picked up the one he'd removed, his own, and put it inside. "Those were way cool pictures."

"You can't talk about these to anyone," I said. "This is proof of a crime, both by the people in the picture and also by the photographer."

Tyler nodded, fiddling with his camera and getting up close to one of the tree skirts and taking a picture. I wasn't at all certain he heard me, but I didn't want to talk too loudly lest someone overhear.

I listened and there were plenty of people talking, enough so that you wouldn't easily pick out another conversation, but if something we said interested someone, well they would hear everything. I hoped that Marci wasn't interested. I leaned out of my booth a bit so I could see around her shelves, and she was sitting in her lawn chair talking to a woman clad in a green velour sweat suit about her mint mocha scented soap. Good. They'd not been paying attention.

Rita was laughing with a woman pushing a stroller, making coo-y voices to the baby. Also good.

If anyone had heard, they were walking along. Now, I had to decide what to do with the pictures. I didn't want to hurt Rita, but clearly she'd been in a car when it hit someone and killed them. The photographer, who I did not know, had been more interested in what was probably blackmail than he was in helping a woman who had been hit. The mayor was more concerned about his career than Penny, who was, technically, an employee of his.

I talked to a few other customers, a young woman who purchased a scarf paying me all in small change, an adult woman I had seen around the neighborhood, who mostly just chatted and then gave in and purchased a tree skirt, and an older man who got very excited about the tree skirts and went to get his wife.

My heart just wasn't in it though. Normally I love talking to people, meeting them, catching up with them, learning about what has happened to them over the year, but at that time the memory disk was always there in the back of my mind, nagging at me.

If I gave it to the chief of police, could he do anything about it? It wasn't like there was a chain of *evidence or anything, and I knew, from watching detective shows on TV, that chain of evidence is very important. Of course, all evidence had to start somewhere.*

It made me wonder who the photographer was.

Denise came by. Tyler wasn't in tow.

"Dad sent me to spell you." Denise said that about the same way she might have spoken when she was seventeen and had better things to do.

"I'll go get something to eat and be back quickly," I said. While some people broke the rules, we really weren't supposed to be eating around the booths.

Denise shrugged and settled back into my chair. I noticed she'd brought her phone and was flipping through Facebook before I even left. Even though she seems like she's completely uninterested, she does do a good job selling, and out of the corner of my eye I saw her stand up and greet a group of people who were just browsing.

I glanced at the booths along the mall, one on either side in front of the shops. I paused a little longer at the photographers. One did landscapes in bright sunlight with super-saturated color. Another did sunsets and sunrises around the city.

I saw someone who did Lexington skylines, someone else who did horses, both at night and in daylight, so I took a card. As I browsed, I thought I recognized a barn. Definitely local.

Not far past the photographer's booth, was the food pavilion where I evaluated my options. They were serving hot dogs, popcorn, and some BBQ ribs. I got the ribs, a small side of baked beans and a sweet tea. I heard the laughter coming from out in the parking lot at the bourbon tasting stand.

I chatted with a couple of other booth owners, Nadine who made beeswax candles and Charlie who did beaded jewelry and ornaments, and found out that their sales had been a bit slower than last year too.

"Of course," Nadine said, "It looks like the crowds are picking up."

She was right. We went and tossed our garbage— fortunately there weren't many ribs on the plate because they were not the best I'd ever eaten—and I caught sight of the young man who had put the memory card in Rita's ball of yarn. He was at the booth I'd paused at just before the pavilion.

"Are you the photographer?" I asked, walking up to him. The sign said *David Paytner, Photography*. He had the familiar horse barn. Of course, they all looked seemed to look alike, particularly at night when they were just a shadow of a broad building with a cupola. While I knew some of his subjects, his photography was competent but nothing spectacular.

"I am," he said. He was a bit older than I first guessed. While his hair was a plain brown, there were lines at the corners of his eyes. His shirt had looked like plain cotton but up close it was something finer. He wasn't just a poor young student as I'd thought.

"These are very nice. You should do more around Arden." I smiled at him, waiting to hear what he'd say.

"I'm working on it, but there are so many other folks doing that. I like Lexington. I can play with night

light so much more there. Around here, it's just dark."
He was still at ease.

"But I'm sure you never know exactly what you'll
get." I wondered whether I should mention that my
grandson loved photography.

David smiled again and looked down at his table.

I sighed. Was my word enough for the police or did
I need more? I started to leave and then thought better
of it.

"Oh," I said turning back. He looked up from
arranging a couple of things on his table. "Did I see
you the other night taking some shots of Main Street
just after they put up Christmas decorations? I'd love
to see some of those shots."

He gave me a tight smile and shook his head. "Took
some but none worked out. I'm used to using a lower
light and touching up because of what I can do with
Lexington shots. I'll do better next year."

I smiled and nodded. I had him. At least I thought
I did. I wished I had been able to record the
conversation but I hadn't bothered to think it through.
Without a recording, it would be his word against
mine.

I hurried back to my booth, noticing Denise was
still chatting. There were more people around. If I
turned in the memory card now I'd probably be stuck
chatting at the station, and I didn't want to do that.
Instead, I smiled at my daughter and settled in.

I talked to dozens of people through the afternoon.
Denise stayed until it was time for Tyler to sing. The

mall area piped in the music so all of us could hear, whether we wanted to or not.

Tyler's class wasn't bad. Not good. Not something I'd want to record. Denise probably would and then force us all to listen on Christmas Eve. I sold out of tree skirts and scarves. By the end of the day, I was starting to open up my box of potholders, which were priced well below Rita's potholders.

As I thought about that, I wondered whether she was also hoping for money from the mayor. After all, she liked money, and she always dressed well above the means of a woman her age with three children and a husband who worked for the power company.

Had she been in it with the photographer? My husband arrived to help me close up. I let him do more than I usually do, although there would be a mess to clean up later, but I was busy watching Rita. She seemed to take an inordinate amount of time with the ball of yarn. I looked around. Marci was mostly done with her things.

My husband got the hand truck to take a load of boxes to the car. It was the perfect time to talk to Rita. There were people around, but not so many as would listen in. Over by the door, a man in the beige and brown uniform of security was helping a woman with an oversized cardboard box. People really ought to learn to pack.

This time I fiddled around with my phone until I figured out how to set it to record. Then I placed it carefully in the pocket of the long sweater I was wearing. I'd crocheted it myself for myself, though if someone asked, I did take orders for things like that. I had two people to correspond with by email after the fair.

"Rita," I said.

She looked up from the yarn balls she was examining. She didn't say anything.

"Are you looking for this?" I held up the memory card.

Rita went to grab at it but I pulled my hand back quickly enough that she missed.

"That's mine. You're nothing but a sneaky little thief!"

"I was picking up the yarn when we talked earlier and I felt this come out in my hand," I said evenly. "I forgot about it until I saw you looking at the yarn." I hoped that my phone could pick up what was said. There was a lot of background noise, squeaks and squawks from the hand trucks and carts and murmured voices.

"That's mine," Rita said, frowning at me, her eyes narrowing.

"I saw that young photographer down at the far end of the mall put it there," I told her, waiting for a reaction.

"He was giving it to me because I paid for it." Rita was still glaring. If she had nothing to hide, you'd think she'd have been nicer to me. It was the sort of misunderstanding that could happen to anyone.

"Blackmail?" I asked.

Rita snorted. "Leave it you to think something salacious."

"Only because I looked at the photos." Mentally I was wondering why she'd say something like that. Did I go after salacious things? I didn't think so. If I were talking about something salacious it was because the facts that I had gathered clearly pointed in that direction.

Rita paled and then her skin reddened with a blush. "Then you know why I want it. The mayor owes me." She spoke softly, almost in a whisper.

"He owes you?" I repeated, hoping that my slightly louder voice would clarify anything the phone couldn't catch.

"He does. He's the one getting everything out of this damned affair. He's a cheap bastard and I want to get my cut before I dump him."

"What about your husband?" I asked. "And the mayor's wife?"

"More sorry for her. She left him. She won't be returning from Florida. I'm not his only bit on the side and I hear his younger gals are getting the goods and I don't mean in the bedroom." Rita was fuming now, her color high. "I'm not some young thing who doesn't know how to make a man sizzle. But does he give me good jewelry? No. I'm the woman he takes places but he doesn't give me things."

I could tell Rita was very upset about not getting gifts.

"You didn't set Penny up, did you?"

"He wasn't supposed to kill her," Rita said softly. "I made sure that area was wet that night. I knew when she walked home, and I thought it would give her a scare if he was a little out of control. I could hold that over him. If we hit her, I figured an ambulance would get there in time. Again, no one would know except David and me."

The photographer, of course.

"Are you having an affair with him too?" I asked. I hated to admit to being shocked but I was. Two affairs? Plus a husband? When did she find the time?

Rita waved me off. "Like you care. David and I like the same things. Good food. Nice clothing. Nice cars. Trips to the big city, and I'm talking places like New York, not Lexington."

As if I needed that education.

"It all takes money," Rita added, as if I didn't know this.

"Which of you hatched the plan?"

Rita narrowed her eyes. "None of your business. I'm certainly not telling you anything more. If you try and take the memory card to the police, I'll let them know what a nosey old bitch you are. I mean who else talks about Willa's baby not being her husband's?"

Besides everyone at the church? Of course, we all had egg on our face when it did turn out to be his, but the skin tone on that child was certainly darker than to be expected.

Rita listed a couple of other little things that I'd known or thought I'd known that turned out to be untrue. She stood there looking triumphant.

I allowed myself to slink back to my table. I kept my phone close, carefully turning off the record button. I finished helping my husband pack up.

In the car, I listened to the recording. It wasn't perfect but clear enough.

"I suppose we need to go to the police station," my husband commented, sighing heavily as if he were put out.

"Of course. It's about being a good citizen. I loved Penny. Many of us did."

"Particularly after she died," my husband said. "Before that you only talked to her if you thought she had some gossip."

I glared. How dared he say that to me?

At any rate, he was good as his word and took me to the police station. He waited inside, reading the old newspaper someone had left in the waiting area. I hadn't told him about the photos, but I told the officer I talked to. Bobby Evans. I remembered when he was in high school, always getting into trouble, but he was a sharp young man. I was happy enough to give him the information.

We were nearly home when the car hit a patch of ice on an otherwise clear road. I felt my throat close up, thinking Rita had done this on purpose. I pictured the car spinning off the road and into the telephone pole nearby, but my husband steered into the skid and got the car under control. We hit no one, although if we had, we would have stopped. It's not like we had anything to hide.

As it was the Christmas season, the second Sunday in Advent, I insisted we go to church the next morning. I was pleased to hear the gossips all talking about how Rita and the mayor had been arrested for the *hit and run accident that had killed Penny Whitesmith. Tongues were definitely wagging about what might have been going on, particularly when I told them about the photographs.*

It wasn't as if I were spreading gossip, you understand. I mean they already knew. I was just making sure they had the story correct.

The Leftovers Club

I was invited to submit a story to an anthology based on holiday secrets. I didn't send this one in. Another one took up all the energy but re-reading it, I quite enjoyed the twists and turns of this particular group of women. For those who like their stories upbeat, this one isn't a happy ending. It is, in fact, a rather depressing tale all around and perhaps the ending is about as happy as it can get for our narrator.

Arlis' basement had transformed from the man cave of a few years back to a girl's club. Gone were the sofas with the drink holders and even the wood paneling. Now, the basement held club chairs that reminded Trish of seashells the way they were formed in a rainbow of pastel colors, all seven of them. The seventh, in a peachy-rose color, was new this year. The others had been there for the last few years.

Clearly there was a new member to the Leftovers Club. That's what Arlis called them. At first it had been Trish and Arlis, both no longer married, both the wrong side of forty, both with kids old enough to create havoc with holiday plans because they never wanted to do what their mothers wanted. When Arlis had invited

Lili, the mother of her son's best friend, Trish had invited a woman from work.

With two more women added in much the same way, the group had grown to six and now there would be seven. Trish wondered who had gotten divorced that year. The holidays were always awkward if you had a family that was now broken.

Trish's younger daughter was in her last year of college and spending the holidays with her roommate. Her older daughter was having Christmas at her in-laws, which was another group of people to juggle.

It seemed that every year, Trish became more and more of a leftover.

Arlis held their annual gathering on Sunday after Thanksgiving. When the kids were younger, it gave the women time to shop on Black Friday and do all the holiday things that were necessary. By Sunday, if the kids were home, they were settled in their rooms texting or gaming or whatever it was that kids did when they hid away in their rooms.

Now, Trish had it on her calendar every year, whether she had the girls for Thanksgiving or not. It was her thing. Trish had brought mixed nuts, a cheese ball, and fancy crackers. Arlis always had wine, the large goblets already out on a tray on the counter of the wet bar over in the far corner from the stairs.

The luxury vinyl plank flooring was mostly gray and made the floor look like it had come from an old shack. The cream and pale green and pink rugs that Arlis had on the floor made the place look like the inside of an easter egg. The old wood paneling was now cream fabric complete with button divots, the buttons in the same pastels as the club chairs.

Arlis had blue Christmas decorations up already. Arlis said it gave her something to do now that her kids were out of the house, a reason to decorate. The blue and gold sparkle balls dangled from blue and gold garland that she had swagged around near the ceiling on small hooks that were up all year round. When it was a dark man cave, Arlis had done the basement in reds, though it had been candy canes and red and silver garland, gold and red looking too much like a football team her husband wasn't fond of.

After setting out the food and pouring herself a glass of the white wine Arlis preferred Trish settled in the eggshell blue chair, her favorite. It put her back to the wet bar so she wasn't distracted by the food. It faced the stairs so she would be ready to greet the women as they came down. Trish liked that.

The women arrived quickly, not quite in bunches, just fast enough to keep Arlis upstairs while Trish sipped the first taste of the dry white. The smell of it almost erased the aroma of popcorn that Arlis had never been able to get rid of in the basement. At least it no longer smelled like beer, which it had the first year, before she'd completely redone the place.

Lili was the last to arrive, with the new woman, she introduced as Laura.

"She's newly divorced. Her husband couldn't deal with the fact that she's a cop," Lili said. Her shoulder length, straight dark hair framed her face. She smiled as if her friend being a cop was a great thing.

Trish shifted slightly uncomfortably. She'd not always had good dealings with the police.

"Nice to meet you all," Laura said, accepting a goblet of the dry white wine that Arlis had started the afternoon with.

Everyone greeted her nicely. Arlis, ever the perfect hostess, asked Laura about her work. Missing persons.

Trish smiled as if that was the most interesting thing in the world, not that she particularly liked police. She pushed away the thought of how they'd treated her older daughter when she'd been accused of shoplifting her senior year of high school. As if all kids didn't get up to such pranks. That was the year Trish had gotten a divorce, so clearly the girl was acting out, yet the police acted as if she were a common criminal, taking her into the station, terrifying her.

Everyone had questions because apparently searching for missing people was the most interesting thing in the world. Trish leaned back in her eggshell blue chair, enjoying the smooth feel of the fabric and sipped her wine, faster, perhaps, than she should have. She didn't care about Laura's work.

In fact, she was becoming annoyed with the woman. They were there to talk about their lives, the lives of their children, the challenges of navigating the holidays when the family was split down the middle. Lili's husband had moved almost a hundred miles away, meaning she had the frustrating chore of meeting him halfway to pick up or drop off the kids. Once, she'd even had to drive it on Christmas Day, which had been hard.

Trish couldn't imagine that. Arlis' husband remained local. And, of course, her kids were near Trish's daughters ages, old enough to drive themselves and make their own decisions. That, however came with its own set of issues.

The first year without her husband, Trish had put up a tree for the girls. After that, they'd gone to their paternal grandparents, not necessarily for their father but to get away from Trish. If they'd gone to her parents, she'd have come along.

The Leftovers Club helped. It was her secret therapy, listening to other women going through the same sorts of pain she'd gone through. She didn't have to spend money she didn't have to talk to a professional but her mind was eased as the holidays approached. She just had to get through Thanksgiving.

This year, she'd ordered the Thanksgiving plate dinner from the local grocery store. Just heat and eat most things, which worked for her. The downside was that there weren't any leftovers, something she'd always loved. But it was better than not having any celebration at all. It was an improvement.

Trish was thankful for the club. She silently toasted to Arlis only to find that her goblet was empty. And Laura was still talking about her work.

It would be bad form to roll her eyes. Trish pushed herself up, biting back the typical groan she often used when she stood now. Once again she was reminded of her age. Laura's skin was still smooth and soft, creamy, almost glowing, despite the fact that there was a hint of tears in the corner of her eyes.

Trish felt her watching her as she got up to refill her goblet. Heard the silence, as Laura paused in whatever story she was telling about a missing person. She bit her lip as she put a few of the crackers and a chunk of cheese on the one of the small plates Arlis had set out. She was drinking too fast. She might just live around the corner, but she still had to walk home.

The neighborhood, with all their sprawling, brick homes and pillared porches, three-car-plus garages hidden around the side, was not the sort of place one went tottering home in. Arlis lived in the house because her husband had let go of it in the divorce, understanding that the prestige that went with it was more important to her than to him. He was a surgeon and therefore eligible for prestige anywhere.

Trish kept the sneer off her face, though only just. Arlis was looking at her funny. No one was talking. Had she said some of that quiet part out loud? She didn't think so. If she had, Arlis would probably be up and screaming at her.

"So how long have you been divorced?" someone asked Laura. "Mine was final just over two years ago."

Trish remembered that first meeting. The woman had cried the entire time. Of course, in her mind, that was better than sharing the details of a rather delicate job like Laura was doing.

Slipping back into her chair, finding the comfortable position, Trish settled in. She set the goblet down so she could munch on some of the cheese and crackers. She noted that Laura had taken some as well and Lili had a brownie. Trish couldn't stand the taste of brownies and dry white wine. The sweetness made the taste far too sour for her but the others seemed to enjoy them.

Arlis even nibbled on one. Leftovers Club Sunday was the one day she allowed herself some sweets, or so she said. It was probably true. Arlis had the figure of a model though she was close to sixty. Her auburn hair was now from a bottle, Trish knew, but everything else was real, even the breasts that stood at attention with merely the help of a good bra, one Arlis swore by. Trish had tried it and she'd noticed her breasts hung down near her bellybutton, so it wasn't just the bra. Arlis worked at keeping anything from sagging. Hell, you could probably still bounce a quarter off her ass.

"I'm not divorced," Laura said.

There were a few gasps. No one was invited to the Leftovers Club unless you were divorced. It was a place of refuge. A secret meeting of the minds on how to get through Christmas without a partner. Why there'd been a woman in the group who'd gotten remarried and although she was still navigating the whole "where will the children go for Thanksgiving and Christmas," because she was remarried and had a partner to help with those sorts of logistics, Arlis had asked her not to return.

Trish remembered there had been a scene. Of course, she'd had plenty of wine by that time and she'd not even been guzzling it. She needed to slow down and eat.

Lili had a boyfriend, but hadn't married him, Trish knew. That was true of several of them. However, boyfriends, and the sort of informal, uncertain commitment, or lack thereof, often just added another layer of logistics. There were decisions about whether he'd be at Christmas with the kids or at Christmas without the kids. In Lili's case, there were his kids, who were still quite young, to deal with as well. No, boyfriends, unlike new husbands, just added to the stress.

Besides, there was always the possibility of a breakup. Of course, Trish reflected, they should also have been aware that there was always the possibility of a divorce. It had happened to all of them.

"My husband died," Laura said. She said it calmly, rather clinically, Trish thought. Perhaps that was her way, being a police officer and all.

"Oh dear," Arlis said, leaning forward. "What happened?"

Trish listened as well. Finally, something interesting.

"He was in a car accident," Laura said. "He was on the highway up towards Hickory. He went off the road. No one even noticed for nearly twelve hours. By then it was too late."

Arlis put a hand to her heart as if this hurt her. The others murmured words of condolence. Lili looked down at the floor, as if having heard the tale before, she was embarrassed to have to sit through her friend's sorrow again.

"You poor, poor thing!" Arlis said, finally. "You need more wine."

Trish noticed that Laura had hardly touched hers. Barely a sip. One of the other women got up to refill her own glass, which required opening a new bottle. She offered more to Laura who shook her head.

"I need to stay alert. I'm back on duty tomorrow."

Arlis nodded. And they started talking about the unique issues of being a police officer and the way the shifts worked and having to juggle children, of which Laura had three.

Trish said nothing. She had nothing to offer.

Laura brought it up.

"Lili told me your husband disappeared and is presumed dead."

Trish froze. She hadn't worked with Laura when she'd reported it. She'd stopped going to the station, begging for them to find him.

"He did," Trish said, looking down at her empty plate. She wondered if it would be okay to set it down and reach for the wine again. She needed it if she were going to have to share her story. Mostly, the others made sure she didn't have to share anything about her husband. She just made a point of avoiding the fact that the kids didn't go with him. They went with his parents.

She hated talking about the fact that he was just gone, perhaps having left her for another woman, but not even having the courage to tell her. Instead, she was left in a strange sort of limbo. The insurance was finally going to pay out so that she'd be able to pay off most of the debt she'd incurred over the last years.

Fortunately, her husband's family had been wealthy and they were loath to see their granddaughters suffer.

Laura nodded, waiting.

Arlis spoke up then. "He left right around the holidays…" she trailed off looking at Trish.

"The day after Christmas," Trish supplied, "In England, I think they call it Boxing Day. He liked to go shopping that day for sales. Not that he needed to shop sales, but his mother had always gone and he liked going. He never came home again."

Laura nodded. "I heard, at the station, that they were looking for a woman they thought met him in the parking lot."

Trish sniffed appropriately, as if she believed her husband had picked up a woman at the after-Christmas fifty-percent-off sale.

"They still talk about it in missing persons?" a friend of Arlis' asked, her voice low, her side-eyed glance at Trish letting Trish know all she needed about how that woman felt about her. She had to admit she didn't like all the women in the group, though they'd been supportive of the various ways in which her life had changed, how she'd become a leftover.

Laura nodded, her eyes still glued to Trish. Trish felt the wine she'd had start to swirl in her belly, rather annoyingly.

"Wow!" Lili said breaking the tension that threatened to swirl in a storm of emotion.

"Wow, indeed," Laura said slowly. "A fisherman pulled up a body, mostly skeleton, from the lake a few months ago. DNA finally came back. It was your husband."

Trish's mouth dropped. She couldn't believe they'd found her husband after all this time. Years, in fact. He was a cold case according to the officer she'd worked with. And no one had told her.

"I can't believe you're springing this on her here rather than in private," Arlis said. Her tone was haughty Arlis, the one that had used to frighten Trish, who had grown up middle class and wasn't used to the ways of the well-to-do. It was only when Arlis had confided that she wasn't actually wealthy, she's just married in, much like Trish, that they'd become friends.

"Maybe it's because we believe she was involved… and had help," Laura said. She stood up, stretching like she was about to go running.

"It's too late to have any cameras but the boat rental places have records and the owner has a thing for faces. He picked out your face, Arlis, as a woman who rented a boat from his company multiple times, one of which was the day after Christmas six years ago, when Trish's husband went missing. Care to say something about that?"

"The Sunday after Thanksgiving, and the day after Christmas are days I go out and make peace with what's going on in my life," Arlis said. "I started that after my husband left me."

"We talked to him," Laura said. "He said you'd been having an affair with a neighbor."

Arlis's face colored slightly. She put a hand to her heart again. Trish felt the wine turning to vinegar in her gut.

The other women were all leaning forward. Lili said nothing. She knew, Trish thought. She knew all along.

"We also talked to your husband's family and your oldest daughter," Laura turned back to Trish. "Usually, you stayed home and cleaned house but that year, you were gone. In fact, the girls started to get worried, you weren't answering your phone. Your husband's parents have always suspected you had something to do with his disappearance because he was threatening to divorce you."

Trish shook her head. "He was, but that's not what happened."

Arlis had pressed her lips together, saying nothing.

"It didn't make sense that the two of you would kill him if Arlis was having an affair with him, so we started considering that two of you might have been having an affair," Laura said quietly.

Gasps from the women.

Trish felt her face color. It had been a brief affair, something that should never have happened. Arlis had moved on, changing lovers of either sex like she changed socks. Trish hadn't found anyone who excited her, nor even made her feel safe the way Arlis had. She'd offered a calm pool in the storm of her husband's periodic outbursts.

"Which one of you actually murdered him?" Laura asked, looking at them.

"I'd like you to leave. And if you won't do that, I'd like my attorney. I assume you're recording this?" Arlis glared at Lili as if this was all her fault. In a way it was. She'd been the one to bring Laura.

Trish wanted nothing more than to run to the bathroom and vomit. She remembered the way Alan had bled all over the car, the time it took to clean it up. She'd called Arlis for help. Arlis always knew what to do. Her friend had suggested the boat, noting how to get the body from the car to the boat so that no one saw exactly what they had. They'd managed to shove him in a box and wrapped it up like a Christmas present, in case anyone had noticed.

Arlis had even artfully decorated the box to look like several smaller boxes of gifts that they were just wheeling out to the large boat all at once. Arlis even knew how to drive a boat, had a license and everything, something Trish didn't have. She'd have been out in her yard digging a hole if not for her friend.

"It was all me," Trish said quietly. Arlis had saved her but now it was her turn to save Arlis. "I did it. I killed him. You're right; he was going to leave me. I was having an affair, but so was he and he was going to leave me for her. It wasn't Arlis. She was just my friend."

Not that Arlis would care about being outed as bi. Half their circle knew by now. But if they were together that would have given Arlis more reason to help her.

"I asked questions hypothetically, after Alan disappeared. And she answered. I did all that. She did rent a boat because I asked her to," Trish said. "And then I went out alone."

That probably wasn't legal but not like accessory after the fact if Arlis had known about the murder.

Arlis's eyes got big. She shook her head a bit. Trish knew that if they had their stories straight no one could figure out which of them had actually wielded the knife. That had been part of the strategy. But this was just Alan. At least they hadn't found Alan's girlfriend who came to the house to confront Trish while he was out. Fortunately, her daughters were out that day. It was why Arlis was with Trish when she killed her husband.

Laura sighed. "You got that," she said into a mike.

Trish glared at Lili. Lili had the grace to look down at the floor not meeting her eyes. Arlis looked defiant.

"I'll call my attorney and have him meet you at the station. Don't say another word," Arlis ordered Trish, though Trish knew it was too late. She'd go to prison. Fortunately, the pills she'd taken with her wine should see that she didn't last long. At least not if she'd been lucky. Then they'd only have her leftover corpse to deal with.

The Advent Calendar Deaths

This tale is a bit more hardboiled than most of the other stories in the collection. Because we're talking about an organized crime family, naturally none of them are good people. But when bad things happen to them, someone has to fix it and make sure it doesn't happen again. The fixer is an unlikely character and, contrary to my adoration of felines, does not actually like cats. I'm sure that's why she's a villain. But don't worry, no cats are harmed in the tale. In fact, other than a few cameo appearances in a house, there are no cats at all.

It was the snowman across the street that did it. While most of Max Krenner's neighbors put up Christmas decorations every year, the house on the corner across the way was always dark. I'd liked that about them. I mean who needs to wrap a hundred thousand lights and a dozen brilliantly glowing reindeer and Santas around the house in a show of holiday spirit? Especially if they had no more of it than I did.

Max, at least, admitted he did it because his wife Elena loved decorating. And Max adored Elena. Not enough, mind, to stay physically faithful, but Max was a rule unto himself. I mean, when you run crime in a city, even a small city like Louisville, you get used to a certain amount of power, and, dare I say, using people.

I'd worked for Max for over a decade since he picked me up on the street when I was trying to steal from him. He'd seen something in me, or rather the limping terrier he'd had at the time saw something in me and Max listened to his dogs. He was probably more bonded to his dogs and cats than he was to his wife. In his legitimate life—yes, he had one of those—he sat on the board of an animal shelter. Currently, I believe the household sat at three dogs, one missing his lower leg, and six cats, all of whom adored him.

Every year he had a Christmas party. Not a holiday party. Other people could celebrate their own holidays. Max celebrated Santa. He loved the idea of someone just coming around and leaving goodies around the house. And so, no matter what someone's religion, they came to the house and celebrated Christmas, but a secular one. I often ended up near the big windows, looking out, making sure the bodyguards around the outside were doing their job, and watching the black hole that was the neighbor's house. It was more interesting than anything else going on. I hated parties but this one was required.

Three years ago, Max had had his usual party, which he held the Friday after the first Sunday in Advent. Don't think that he doesn't know the

Christian calendar down to the hour, raised as he was, though he rejects that just like he rejects a lot of other things most people hold dear. The woman who lived in the house across the way had come over to join in, sans hubs. And she hadn't left until the next afternoon, her hair messed and her dress askew, smelling of multiple rounds of rough sex and sporting a smile that suggested she'd liked it.

Not Max for a change—though he'd had plenty of affairs—but Sam, Max's bodyguard. Max's wife, Elena told me what had happened after the other woman's walk of shame down the long, curving drive and across the meandering street where the smell of the river coated the air like fog. The wife, whose name I never knew, had packed a bag and gotten in her Mercedes, and driven off, filing for a divorce from Nevada where she'd heard that it was easier to obtain one.

I'd never met Neil, her husband but I pictured him as a sort of tall, skinny, nerdy type who didn't know how to satisfy a woman. I was wrong about his looks but probably not much else.

That was three years ago. The last two years on Christmas Eve, the day Advent ends, the body of a woman had been found inside one of those air-filled snowmen somewhere in Louisville. The husband typically lived within a few homes of the find. The police did what they could to keep details quiet, so it was only after Elena disappeared and Max started getting links to a very special Advent Calendar that I learned what had gone on.

Elena was taken on the first day of Advent. If it went on as in previous years, every day for the season of Advent the husband of the woman taken would get a link to an advent calendar video. Max's had the theme of a couple in a sleigh in a nice Christmas Village, but I had heard the first one used Santa, his elves, and Rudolph, with the only odd thing being a drop (or more as days went on) of blood on the ground. The last image would always be the wife being hurt in some way.

In Max's calendar, there had been images of a happy couple riding slowly through a quaint snowy village. When the camera zoomed in on it, a single drop of blood had dripped on the pristine white snow. The final image was an image of a dark van with Elena getting dragged into it by a shapeless shadow.

Day two showed the couple on the steps of the church as if going in. At the end, Elena was superimposed there, her nose dripping blood, her face bruised, tears flowing.

Day three, while the couple held onto papers and sang into the night, the last image featured Elena doubled over, her mouth open as she gasped in pain, but she was set to appear as if she, too, were singing.

Max, of course, called all of his less-than-legitimate workers to the house. My ragged Ford Fiesta that fit into the kinds of neighborhoods where I lived and worked stood out in the ritzy area my employer lived. I was used to that. Didn't care. The people there often looked askance at it but the police knew better than to stop one of Max's employees.

Max had an office downtown for legitimate business and a warehouse not far from my apartment for everything else. The office wasn't large enough for the group and Max didn't want everyone meeting at the warehouse which would draw attention to the fact that he owned it and used it.

I took care of warehouse stuff. Max's sense of humor had run to having me trained in all sorts of martial arts so that at barely five foot and just over a hundred pounds I got to order around all his thugs. And, devious man that he was, he needed a loyal female to snitch on Elena if she started keeping secrets. I wasn't Elena's bodyguard or her confident, though I knew my job was to chat her up whenever I was in the house.

I didn't dislike her, which is saying something for me. She was good with the cats and the dogs and seemed to adore them as much as Max did. The dogs sometimes liked me, sometimes ignored me. Max's fat gray and white cat with the missing ear insisted upon sitting on my lap whenever I sat down. As a result, I rarely sat down. The sound the cat made, that rumble in its chest made me antsy though I knew others found it calming.

It was during the meeting that I'd been standing at the dining room window, looking out over the neighborhood when I noticed the snowman. All of the other women had been found in a neighbor's yard in an inflatable snowman. Never before had Neil, before or after his wife had left, put up any decorations. This year it wasn't just the snowman but a Santa and reindeer and I even noted where lights were lined up along the roofline.

"You get new neighbors?" I asked Max.

"Where?" Max didn't bother to look up. He was studying the image that had just come in as if the snowy village would give him some clue as to where in Louisville—which had no snow at all—Elena was being held. Max's most important people had seats around the table. The rest of us could get chairs lined in around behind. I stood. Avoiding the cat, of course.

The dogs had taken their places near Max's feet, under the table, perhaps hoping to get a treat. Of the cats, only the gray and white cat waited in the living room, watching us. I was certain it was watching me, waiting for me to sit.

"Across the way. The guy who never decorates has decorations up," I said.

"What does it matter?" Irwin snapped. Irwin was Max's right hand, his secretary, his computer genius who did all the sketchy techy work that needed to be done.

"There's a snowman. And other stuff. The neighbor has to see it." I waited for them to get where I was going.

"So?" Irwin snapped. He can be dense about street stuff. It's kind of amazing he's still alive, really.

"The neighbor has to see it. Has to know. There are even lights on the eves. If nothing has changed, why? It has to be related to Elena being taken." We'd plowed through the police records, some they gave us when Max reported his wife missing, some Irwin found for

46

us. We all knew that the other neighbors had put up the snowmen themselves and had been horrified that it was used that way. All had used the same decoration in past years.

"You think someone put him up to it?" Max asked.

"Or he's our guy," I said. "Either way, I think Sam and I ought to pay him a visit."

Max's bodyguard Sam was at least six two and was about three times my weight. He could probably pick me up with one arm if he had to—and I let him, which probably wouldn't ever happen unless I was dead. Even unconscious I'd probably bite. I do not like to be touched.

I might do the actual dirty work, but Sam looked tough. And, in this case, I wanted to look tough, not harmless enough to get close for the killing blow.

Sam and I walked over. No sense in taking a car that might be noticed. While Sam drives a Beamer sports car, it usually sits at Max's. While the police might not bother us, I knew they made note of what went on at Max's. Just in case.

Plus, while I was willing to use their information, their sources, to get us closer to Elena, I wasn't willing to trust her life to them. I mean, come on. This was Louisville—although Elena did have being a white woman who met the cultural standards of beauty on her side.

The day was colder than usual, a slight breeze blowing in off the river which was about half a mile away. The breeze, naturally, brought the usual river stink to my nose as we walked down Max's drive, which curved down from the house to the street, the creamy white cement without a single blemish on it. Max's lawn was still perfectly green, though I couldn't have said how he did it. A fortune in chemicals, probably.

He had four trees off to the side, where the road curved slightly, cuddling his house close. Two had only skeletal branches. The other two were hearty evergreens that towered over their spindly companions. Large bushes filled in the rest of that side. Low bushes lined the front side nearest the driveway entrance.

I heard a car start a few houses down, and the mournful call of a tug. From far away I heard kids laughing at recess at the local school which backed up to part of the neighborhood. Not far as the crow flew but by road it took almost fifteen minutes to get there. This particular neighborhood liked its winding curves and blind dead ends, framed by houses with landscaping fluffed and prepped until it seemed more like a living breathing thing than a neighborhood.

In all the years I'd known Max and all the times I'd been to the house, I'd never once seen a single squirrel, though you'd think they'd love the trees and bushes around. I saw more life down by the warehouse with the jays in the summer and even the occasional rat that wandered out of the shadows. I'd take my warehouse district over Max's neighborhood any day. At least I recognized the people around me for what they were.

Neil's driveway led straight up into a garage that sat slightly behind the huge rectangular box of a red-brick house that was as appealing as the warehouse I often worked in. At least in my mind, the warehouse was interesting with scuffs and scrapes and missing panels here and there. The paint was uneven and when the kids got going with the graffiti it could be downright artistic—if you thought "Your Mother Sucks Dick" was artistic.

This house was plain. No porch graced the front, not a single column broke up the brick. Nothing stuck out here or there, no bay window broke up the façade. Just plain rectangular windows all uniform in size, shutterless.

Even the landscaping was dull, the grass yellowing from the cold nights and the lack of water we'd had this past year. A single tree stood bare-branched, alone towards the side nearest the house next door. The other side bordered a road that took people out of the neighborhood by a winding and unpopular path. That was where Neil had put most of his decorations, perhaps to keep them at arm's length if Elena's body was to be found in the snowman.

I sniffed the air but got only a lungful of river stink. Not a hint of Elena's perfume, though she wouldn't have gone in and out of the house for several days and probably not by the front door. While the garage was set back from the house, it was attached.

I pulled out my phone and texted Irwin. I wanted to know if Neil had a van registered in his name. I didn't care about the color. Color could be changed. Especially if you had the kind of money it took to live in this neighborhood.

Sam banged on the door while I was writing. No one answered. I wasn't surprised. We walked around the side of the house, up the driveway, which was cream cement like Max's, but that was where the resemblance ended. Next to the house, the cement was cracked and worn, though the area most people would see looked smooth.

Neil only took care of things where people could see. Probably why his wife left three years ago.

The garage had no windows to look through. The house looked unlived in. The place was on a hill sloping down behind so there was likely a basement. Max had had a basement built in, though no one liked to do that around that area thanks to the water table. However, you never knew when you might need to hide something. I had a feeling the interior of Max's place had a hidden room somewhere as well, perhaps a safe room or perhaps a room used for other things, and the damp basement was a ruse.

Max was like that. I loved that about him.

I felt my phone buzz in response to my text. Irwin's note said Neil didn't have a van but his company did. Irwin pointed out that although Neil didn't own the company, he was a high-level manager and could probably take a company vehicle if he needed it for a short time with few questions asked. The vans were dark gray.

I showed the response to Sam.

"I'll break down the door," he said.

"Think she's here?" I asked.

Irwin would be getting information on where Neil worked, important things like other homes, whether the company had warehouses that might not be in use just then.

"Yeah," Sam said. "That video shit takes work. I tried doing a video for a girlfriend once. Took me days. If he's using images of the women in them, and the police said that in later ones the women move, he's got to spend time doing all that editing stuff. And finding the images, you know? Planning it. He'll be doing a lot of that at home. Besides, the last few years—everyone worked at home."

Sam was right. He wasn't just a pretty bit of muscle. Which would be why Max kept him around.

I let him pick the lock while I eyed the surroundings. Nothing out of the ordinary, other than the upscale crap that gave me itchiness in a neighborhood like this, although I did note that Neil's crap was less than perfectly cared for. Like the driveway near the house, the side yard looked slightly unkempt. The paint on the door had begun to peel and I noticed part of the eves hung down lower than the rest a few inches from the corner of the house. Even the Christmas lights stopped at the edge of the front of the house.

My fingers twitched as I thought about the items that were probably inside. Like opening a Christmas present. Of course, if Elena wasn't there, I wouldn't be taking anything. And if Elena was there, I wouldn't be taking anything because I'd be busy killing Neil.

A car drove by outside, but neither Sam nor I let it bother us as he opened the door and let us in. A bit slower than I'd have been but Sam had other uses.

The floor creaked when Sam stepped inside. It didn't make a sound when I walked in, closing the door softly behind us. Sam had stopped moving and was listening. We were in one of those smallish entrances that made up mud rooms. Coat hooks hung off to the side and there were spaces for shoes, though so far as I knew, only Neil lived there and he hadn't left any shoes. He had two jackets on hooks, though.

A door off to the right led into a long narrow room that probably went to the garage. It also held the washer and dryer. The floor in the mudroom and the laundry was scuffed tile with blue flecks. Like the outside of the house, while this was high-end stuff, it hadn't been well cared for. I suspected the time on the lack of care was approximately three years.

Sam stepped carefully, avoiding any sounds of his movement, and opened the door to the main part of the house. It looked like an outside door with a glass panel set in it, like an airlock or an addition, though I couldn't see where the addition began and the main part of the house ended.

The HVAC clicked on when I moved and I froze in place. The warm air spilled down from a vent above Sam's head in what ended up being the kitchen that stank of bleach. Bad sign.

Neil's kitchen was almost as large as Max's but, like so much else, it looked neglected. The shine on the stainless fridge was marked with so many fingerprints it looked a bit like a child's finger painting in gray on silver.

The faucet over the sink, under the back window to my right, dripped, slowly but steadily. Dishes were stacked next to the faucet and I itched to see if I could shut it off. The drip annoyed me and kept me from being able to listen for odd sounds.

Sam walked across the room and looked behind a door. He nodded at me. Stairs, then, to the basement I figured existed. I hurriedly followed. The bleach stink got stronger the longer I was in the room. I'd snuck into public pools that didn't smell as much.

Sam was halfway down when I started to follow. I heard nothing in the basement at first. But then a faint knock. It was almost too regular to be human but then it would stop for a moment. I could still hear the HVAC, so it wasn't that.

Like Max's basement, this was concrete with no finishings. The large room that we landed in had a big window off to my right giving me a view of the backyard. It was rather odd to look out and see the dirt and dust and detritus that had blown up against the window in the fall. It made the room dimmer than it needed to be.

I pulled out my phone to use as a flashlight. Sam turned on the overhead not caring if we were noticed.

The knocking sound came from straight ahead. A door was slightly off to the left and Sam opened it, flinging it open and stepping to the side. I was already flat against the wall away from the door.

No one shot at us. I hadn't seen a car and suspected Neil was off at work or perhaps just running an errand to set Elena up for her next video.

Sam reached in and flipped a light switch. Four spotlights came on and lit the room up like a crime scene. Which, seeing that Elena was tied to a cot that appeared to be bolted to the wall, it was.

Sam rushed over to untie her and get her out of there. I took photos and sent them to Max.

Neil was not long for this world, but I wasn't quite sure how I wanted to do it. I had my knife, but that seemed a little fast for him. Max sent a note that I ought to take care of it and have Sam bring Elena home.

I was, after all, Max's fixer. Sam slipped out with Elena. I followed upstairs after turning out the lights. Then, I settled into a chair in Neil's living room. It had been a nice chair once, but now it was threadbare. The seat sank into a shape that didn't fit me at all. I suspected it was the shape of Neil's ass.

Sam had barely gotten across the street when I heard a car pull into the driveway. I smiled to myself, fingering my blade. I hadn't had to wait long.

Before the door opened, the smart home system turned on Christmas carols. This one was a man laughing to the tune of Jingle Bells and set my teeth on edge before the first verse was done. If I knew where he kept the speakers, I'd have smashed them, but I hadn't gone looking for those. Until now, I hadn't cared.

Irwin would make sure any security cameras and tapes were fixed before we called the police, which would be well after Neil had been taken care of.

And if I was wondering if he really did have surveillance in his house, Neil came at me poised and ready for a fight. As always, men underestimated me. Neil made a bull's run at me and I sidestepped. I can carry a knife in either hand, so I used the one he rushed by to slice at his torso. That brought him to an unceremonious halt.

He turned glaring at me.

Rather than being tall and thin, Neil was barely average height with a slight paunch in his belly and ugly looking with a nose that was too wide for the rest of his narrow face. His mouth was thin, almost cruel and there were no lines that suggested he ever smiled. When I looked into his eyes, I saw something even deader than what I saw in my own on the rare times I stared into a mirror.

"What the hell?" he muttered under his breath. It was hard to hear over the laughing Jingle Bells.

"Only an idiot would take Elena Krenner," I said quietly.

"It was Max's fault my wife left," Neil said. "He needs to pay!"

"What about the women from the last two years?" I asked. I really was curious. There was something sad about this man, like watching a body loaded onto an ambulance after a car accident I hadn't caused.

Neil shook his head. "They were practice. I wanted to get it right. I wanted it to be perfect. It was all for Elena!"

"Idiot." I muttered. I didn't move.

Neil came to me, thinking I was small and he could grab my wrist and take the knife.

Like before, I moved easily out of his way considering how far in advance he telegraphed his moves. I had to hop on the chair I'd been sitting on before he'd come home, but I didn't worry about that. It was so old there were no doubt tons of forensic evidence that had nothing to do with me.

Besides, Max had probably already called someone to sterilize the room. They'd be there in an hour or so. Max was good with timing.

I turned and waited for Neil to come at me again. He did.

The man was definitely a middle manager and not a killer. It was no wonder he'd had to practice. I slammed the knife into the side of his neck without a problem and blood spurted. I tried to get out of the way but it hit me hard in the face.

My lack of goggles and mask annoyed me. You can't be too careful anymore. At least Max offered decent health insurance and a good retirement plan if I caught something on the job. I twisted the knife and pulled it out, moving out of the way of the spray.

I leaped off the chair, which, fortunately, was not a rocker. I am not a superhero to manage to hold steady even while rocking. I'd have fallen on my ass if I'd tried that.

Neil hadn't lingered dying as long as I'd have liked but he wasn't much of a challenge. Besides, having killed him, I could find the damn speakers and murder that stupid carol. The laughing was giving me a headache.

That done, I pulled out my phone and texted Max. Asked him to put Neil in the snowman. Blood pooled at my feet. I considered having Irwin make a final Advent Calendar entry with Neil bleeding out but that would be a little too cute. I had a feeling the police wouldn't like that. The body in the snowman, however, could have been done by anyone.

I wiped blood from my face so at least I wasn't dripping. It was getting towards dusk. I made sure there wasn't any traffic coming down the street and jogged over to Max's. If any neighbors happened to look out, they'd probably have thought I was wearing an elf shirt or something. The houses were very far apart.

"Get cleaned up," Max snarled when I entered the house. "You're a mess."

I shrugged but did as he asked. There's a bathroom for the bodyguards and a place I could change. The clothing would be too big as they were all toughs and thugs who were closer to Sam's size than mine, but it would do.

Once refreshed, I stepped out, thinking about the first time I had killed for Max. I'd been a blubbering mess. But that had been a very long time ago.

"Nice idea about the snowman. Irwin's already fixed the security footage at the house," Max said when I finished and checked into his office. A large orange cat sat on his lap. Max absently rubbed its ears. A black lab, this one with eyes glazed from age lay at his feet.

The other two dogs weren't around. "Elena is safe thanks to you."

I nodded at him, waiting.

"How's Elena doing?" I finally asked.

"The dogs are with her. They'll perk her up. I'll have a doctor come by later."

It must be nice to be so rich you could have a doctor come by. I'd been worked on by Max's doctor, too. I liked her better than some of the ones I'd run into on routine checkups. She didn't beat around the bush or ask intrusive questions about lifestyle. I must have been lost in thought because when I next looked at Max, he had an envelope in his hand and was passing it over.

"Christmas bonus," Max said. I noticed that in addition to money there was a ticket.

"What's this?" I looked up at him.

"Ticket to Aruba. Get some sun. Make sure you're not around when the police find the asshole's body. I'll see you in February."

I glared at the ticket. I hate to travel. Hadn't done much. I wouldn't own a passport if Irwin hadn't created one for me under a name that wasn't my own. On the bright side, at least it would get me out of Max's annual Christmas party. I wouldn't have to stand around avoiding the damned gray and white cat this year.

The Best Christmas Ever

What's a holiday crime anthology without a murder at a holiday party? I'm a big fan of the trope that whoever dies has to be the bad guy in the tale. Perhaps it's my reading of cozy mysteries where the murder happens off the page and the person is always, always horrible. That's true here, too. And while Patten isn't a nice person, either, it's hard not to root for her in this particular tale. In fact, she may turn up in another mystery or two. Because her career isn't over.

Screams echoed around the large room despite the too loud Christmas music playing in the background. For a party billed as a winter holiday party, they'd gone all out with the Christmas theme. A tree that had to be at least twelve feet sat off to the side with blue and green round ornaments of the sort that come six to a package. Bright red and white garland hung on the edges and white twinkle lights gave a light strobe effect in the low lights around the huge room, garland draped and sagging along the walls near the ceiling.

It smelled of slightly overdone roast beef and too much wine, which had probably been spilled, though no one walked around with a shirt or dress covered in red stains like blood. If there'd been a spill it had landed safely on the carpet, which given the blues, burgundies, and blacks of the pattern would probably never notice another splash of burgundy.

The huge room was the main room of the party, with windows overlooking the parking lot and the trees beyond. Not exactly a stunning view. Not a single window opened, though the room was stuffy with the heat of bodies becoming ripe as they fermented the wine in their bellies and sweat it back out.

A wall of doors opened onto a gathering area at the foot of the basement stairs and the party had taken over that space as well, probably because it was a little cooler out there, away from the hot food, and the toasts and talks. Or maybe it was just the one place someone could flop on a sofa rather than perching on the uncomfortable conference chairs that were scattered around now that the round tables had been pushed aside.

Patten drifted slowly towards where the crowd was converging, both hands gripping her glass of wine, though hers was white. Her long fingernails had been painted red and had snowflakes and little snowmen covering them. She'd had fake nails put on, their tips longer than she was used to, hence the need to carry the wine with both hands.

It wasn't like she cared about the gauzy navy blue dress she was wearing. She'd gotten it cheap figuring it would look nice enough in dim light and it wasn't as if she would wear it again. The company like to pretend it was high class when in actuality it was anything but.

The women around her wore too many sequins or too much black. Hair was puffed up around their heads so high that they were all taller than the men. Patten wasn't sure she'd ever seen such big hair in her real life before. They were all throwbacks to another era in their taste.

The men wore suits, most of them ill-fitting. Kyle from accounting had an actual gray suit that fit though he'd tugged at his Santa tie so hard it was coming unknotted. His color looked good, so unlike so many others he hadn't over-indulged. Probably a good thing. His suit probably cost some money unlike the off-the-rack things most of the men were wearing.

Pushing her way through the small crowd, Patten looked down upon Vincent Benson, the CEO. He was lying partly on his side and partly on his back as someone attempted to do CPR and another knelt near his head. Dispassionately, Patten noticed they weren't doing it right.

One of her tiny snowflakes came loose from her fingernail and she looked at, frowning. To be honest, she was more upset about the manicure than she was about the boss. He'd been an ass. If he wasn't the boss, he'd have been fired for sexual harassment. As it was, the police had investigated him multiple times, though none of the complaints had ever had any witnesses and Vincent had continued doing his thing, ignoring the looks and the whispers.

Patten drifted away. She'd spent a lot of money on the manicure. More than on the dress. Probably more than she could have afforded. The job didn't pay that well. In fact, the pay was the second worst thing about the job after Vincent.

But her sister had gotten her the job and it wasn't something Patten could turn down. She definitely needed the money.

There was a reason Patten knew this party was anything but high class, why she could have put the dresses the women around her wore at the sale rack at the local department store, and why she could recognize a cheap off-the-rack suit versus one that had been professionally tailored to fit, though not bespoke.

Her credit cards were maxed and she'd had a dry spell in terms of finding work. This paid some of the bills. She crashed at her sister's. Kept her updated on what was happening at the company and generally made plans. Patten had big plans.

She settled herself at a reasonable distance from the crowd and watched everyone. It didn't take long for the EMTs to arrive and take over for the people attempting to save Vincent Benson's life.

"Do you think he had a heart attack?" someone asked.

"What else?" a man said.

"Maybe he got handsy with the wrong woman," the first speaker said.

Patten glanced up at them. She was blonde with her hair teased at least three inches above her brow. Her sequined mermaid dress was a half-size too small and her breasts threatened to spill out of the top, which, thinking about it, was probably the point. The man next to her was in a black suit with frayed cuffs with jacket buttons that didn't quite reach around his girth. It had, no doubt, been purchased a dozen years and two sizes ago.

The one thing she could say for the company was that it didn't have a ton of turnover. Not that there were tons of jobs around the area. The engineers were might come and go, joining the place from out of town to get something on their resume, but most everyone else was local. It was the largest employer around. And now the CEO and owner was laying on the floor being treated by the EMTs.

Patten suspected he'd be dead shortly, if he wasn't already. The bluish cast to his face did not bode well. Or maybe that had been the twinkle lights. She couldn't be certain.

A tall, thin man dressed in the hotel's uniform pushed his way inside and looked around, trying to ascertain whether they would liable. Probably not, although if poison were found in Vincent's system, perhaps their kitchen workers would be questioned.

The mid-level hotel was the nicest in town. Not exactly saying much considering they were well outside the bounds of Lexington. Even Lexington wasn't exactly the big city where the rich and beautiful would dance and party and eat something better than slightly overcooked roast beef.

Patten remembered crab legs. Even shrimp was better than the rubbery stuff that they served as beef at the buffet which was now closed. Desserts still lined tables but the hot food was finished. It had been mostly gone, no matter that it wasn't that good. Most of the people working there probably wanted to get their money's worth on a free meal. It was one of the few perks Vincent allowed his employees.

The year-end bonus was a gift-card to Target, valued between $10 and $100 depending upon the position and the seniority. Patten expected hers would be $10. She'd use it, she had no doubt. There were always things she could find at Target. Too bad the nearest one was in Lexington, which was a good forty minutes away. It might cost some of the employees that much money in gas to get there in their big old trucks.

Still, it was a job. She reminded herself of that. Even if Bree wasn't her sister, it was a job worth doing.

A blue-uniformed cop came in and looked around. Patten made eye-contact. Just another employee hanging around to find out what had happened. She fiddled with her extra-long nails. Maybe she should have gotten them shorter. But then again, her manicurist knew what she was doing.

Radio static burst through the music, which someone turned off. Though whispers traveled around the room and some people were still talking in the other room, not yet aware, or too drunk to care, what was happening the main room of the event, the place felt silent without the warm wrapping of the music.

Several other officers arrived. The EMTs were standing back. Vincent hadn't even made it to the hospital. Patten made a face.

"He said his drink tasted funny," Mrs. Vincent Benson was saying. No one knew her first name. The joke was that it was "Missus" as that was all that was ever used.

"Is the glass around, ma'am," the officer asked.

Someone found a glass on the floor. There was no way to be certain if it was the glass that Vincent had drank from. It was empty, too, the wine having spilled all over the floor. He'd been drinking white like Patten. It was one reason she'd picked up the white. Well, that and the fact that she didn't want to spill red down her dress as the revelers became a bit less inhibited.

"He was arguing with Lance Wingate," another person pointed out.

Patten knew Lance. He worked in HR. He'd been the one to hire her for the receptionist position. Lance had a tendency to be over cautious about speaking to people. Patten usually sat in on personnel issues if Myra Lowen wasn't there. Myra worked as Lance's assistant.

Lance was standing there in a blue pin-striped suit that nearly fit him. It was a little lose around the shoulders but the length was good as was the fit through the waist, which was a sticking point for so many. The pants brushed the tops of his scuffed shoes just the way they should. Patten could forgive him for not wearing shiny shoes with the suit. These were clearly comfortable.

Everyone had stood a little too much that evening. Even her feet, so often used to her punishing days, were tired of from the high heels she was wearing.

"Mr. Wingate," one of the officers said taking him aside. Lance looked nervous. Patten had a feeling there would be sweat stains on his suit jacket, requiring it be dry-cleaned. Lance would make sure that was done promptly. He was very careful.

And not a murderer.

Patten knew he'd often been tasked with talking to his boss, the owner of the company about the problems with sexual harassment. She also knew, having listened in, that Vincent thought it was funny that Lance worried about such things.

"What are they going to do? Fire me?" Vincent said. "I'm always careful that no one sees me. They can't prove a damned thing if no one sees me."

Lance tried to explain that things were different now but Vincent wouldn't hear it.

It was that conversation that had made up her mind.

Bree had left the company, losing out on unemployment because she'd quit, but Vincent had made it impossible for her to stay. Bree had gone to school to be an engineer on a scholarship from Vincent's company and as such had agreed to work there for three years after she graduated. She'd made it exactly three.

Unfortunately, Vincent wasn't giving her a good reference and interested employers would often talk about references and then not call her back. A friend of a friend of a friend had managed to get through the cone of silence to find out what was happening. It was Vincent.

The original idea had been to have Patten there as the receptionist to offer references for anyone calling. Good references for anyone who had left because of Vincent.

But Patten had other talents and she'd used them well.

She didn't listen at doors. She planted listening devices. Her sister wasn't the only one good at technology.

Why, that was the whole reason Patten had gotten invited to a very high-end party in Chicago one year. She'd listened in and made sure she was in the right dress at the right place at the right time to have one of the invitees ask her to go with him when his girlfriend stormed off. She'd heard he'd been cheating. Patten might have planted that story, too, but it had gotten her what she wanted. And she'd wanted to be at that party. There were people there she wanted to meet.

Having met them, her bank account had stayed flush for some time. Then Covid hit which took its toll on her finances. Which meant she was looking for a job when Bree had been laid off leading to the whole charade.

Patten wasn't thrilled about being back in Kentucky. She wasn't interested in horses and her preferred drink was tequila, not bourbon. Derby pie would put fat on her body just by looking at it and the idea of a hot brown turned her stomach, though there was a time when she was a child when she'd have eaten one. In fact, she'd gotten sick not long after eating one which might have been the reason for her aversion.

All in all, Kentucky didn't have much for her. This winter, the anemic snows weren't even enough to get excited over. The light dusting she'd seen a week ago wouldn't even have counted as frost in Chicago or New York, though it might have shut down the city in LA.

Those were the kinds of places Patten loved and she hoped to be back to one of them soon enough. She'd already packed up her listening devices, in case the place was closed after Vincent's demise.

There were tears around her, for the people who had realized that Vincent was dead. As if most of the women were that sad. Patten tried to keep her face neutral and concerned looking. That was who she was. Someone who cared that they could talk to. Mostly it had worked.

"They're saying Lance might have poisoned him!" Doreen told her. Doreen's hair was mousy brown but teased up around the top of her head. It was cut short enough that Patten wasn't certain where the height came from but height it had. Doreen's dress was probably a size too large and hung on her, showing off the fact that her breasts were nearly touching her bellybutton.

"Really?" Patten asked, willing her to go on. She hoped that Lance wasn't charged. She'd feel badly about that. Lance was a decent enough guy even if he couldn't get rid of Vincent.

"That's what I heard. I was there when he collapsed. Lance was telling Vincent that he shouldn't have been putting his hands on Kaylee's behind like that and Mrs. Benson was near tears. Vincent, of course, took that badly and was shouting at him when he keeled over. Whatever the poison was, it must have been fast acting."

Actually, it didn't work that fast, Patten knew. In fact, it had worked faster than she'd expected. She could have used a smaller amount, dumped quickly into his drink. That would have saved her some money and made her evening easier.

"It wasn't Lance," someone else said, coming by. Patten wasn't sure of his name. He was probably one of the engineers. He slurred his words only slightly and he was standing straight, though it seemed to be an effort.

"How do you know?" Patten asked. She told herself not to be nervous. No one could have figured out what she'd done. She was good. Vincent wasn't her first murder, although he was the first for which she wasn't being paid, well paid.

"Lance wouldn't kill someone," the man said. "I bet it was that wife of his. How much can one woman put up with?"

Doreen was nodding carefully. Patten gave a non-comital response. She'd rather see Mrs. Benson go down for the murder than Lance, but it wasn't up to her.

A speaker squealed and squawked.

"Listen up, everyone. Anyone from Vincent and Vincent Corporation, we need you to have a seat. We'll be doing interviews and then you'll be on your way home," a voice said. Patten couldn't quite see the person speaking.

The flow led her to a table where she sat, pushing her wine glass away. She had her phone with her so she played with that. She worked a crossword puzzle on her app, only half-listening to the people at her table. Doreen was there but so were seven other people, the tables seating eight.

She listened as rumors swirled. They got more ridiculous as the night wore on. Patton rubbed her neck.

"You're probably sore from looking at your phone all this time," Doreen said, nodding at her, certain that she knew something Patten didn't.

Or her neck might be sore because she had to wait all this time when she really wanted to be home having a bath before heading off for a larger city.

Patten doubted that police from such a small town would think to finger her. She was smarter than they were, having gone off to college and then taught herself a few things on her own. Working in an office was so boring.

Finally, the police got to Patten's table. She was the third person to go into the little conference room the police were using to interview guests.

She looked up to see the plain clothes detective on the case. Mick Dawson. The name was familiar.

"Angelina Patterson, who goes by Patten," Dawson said quietly. "Kentucky is a long way from LA. And I can't see that Vincent and Vincent is exactly the kind of company that you normally work for. Don't you normally work sales?"

Patten tried to relax. They hadn't had anything on her in LA. Just because a jewelry store owner who was acquitted of substituting lower end diamonds in solitaire rings once they were sold had died quickly at a party. That had been a summer party at a private house.

"I've worked a lot of positions. I was here to help out my sister who recently lost her job."

"At Vincent and Vincent," Dawson said.

Patten nodded.

"What's up with that name anyway? I've always wondered," Dawson asked conversationally.

"According to HR, Vincent's father's name was Vincent as well and he didn't think Benson and Sons was unique enough for the company he was founding," Patten said. It was on the HR brochure.

Dawson nodded.

"Y'all must be good if you have my previous employment in LA," Patten said.

Dawson smiled. "I'm good at my job. Besides, I lived in LA at one time. HR mentioned you had been hired a few months ago from LA."

"If not for Bree, I wouldn't have left LA," Patton said. It was probably the truest statement she'd made to the detective, though the others weren't untrue, just that she didn't have much feeling about them.

"Got tired of the rat race in LA. Besides, I'm Kentucky born and bred. Louisville. But my wife and I liked this town better," Mick responded easily. "I got tired of homicide but here I am, investigating another one."

"But…" Patten stopped herself. She wasn't supposed to know too much. And if she asked how he knew it was homicide, she might give herself away.

"You wanted us to think it was just a sudden death. In fact, the rest of the force thought so to. I, however, had seen this before. Once at a party where a certain Angelina Patterson was attending. And the coroner there managed to find traces of poison in the vic's system that time. We couldn't quite trace where it had come from. I'm betting we find the same traces in this vic's system."

Patten slowed her breathing. This was bad. Very, very bad. She had no intention of sitting in jail on Christmas. She had gifts to purchase for her sister and her sister's kids. She'd gotten an inquiry on the coded site she used for that very purpose, accessible only through the dark web. There was a job over New Year's in Boston. It would pay enough to send her to Bahamas for the winter.

"It's really horrible that I've been at parties where two people have died, but I assure you they have nothing to do with me," Patten said.

"Your manicurist in LA was picked up on unrelated drug charges about six months after you left LA," Dawson said. "Explained what you had asked for…"

Patten looked him directly in the eye. She didn't tap her fingernails. Barely breathed. She merely cocked her head, hoping to look innocent. This manicurist had been a bit more creative. No more little opening under the fake nails. This manicurist had placed the poison in a snowman that looked painted on. The snowman had flaked off and dissolved with the rest of the poison in the drink.

"Let me see your nails," Dawson ordered.

Patten held out her hands. "I hope you like them."

He had a technician look at her fingernails. Patten moaned pathetically as they pulled off the too long nails to look under them, hoping to find a secret compartment in one of them. Which, of course they didn't.

Dawson glared at her.

"Have them tested," he said. He wrote something down on a slip of paper.

He glared at Patten who sat there looking at him as innocently as possible. With any luck she'd managed to pick off any white flakes that might have been left over.

She was taken down to the station, ordered to surrender her passport, but let go. They had nothing on her but suspicion. In fact, she could probably have an attorney argue that she hadn't given them permission to remove her lovely nails. But that was for another day.

Instead of fleeing as she wanted to do, Patten went about Christmas shopping. The kids were fun to buy for even if she didn't have a ton of money. Her sister was less fun but she still found something she could wrap and put under the tree.

All the while she waited to see what the results were.

The weeks went by and Patten began to wonder if Dawson was toying with her, perhaps building a case not only against her for Vincent but for L.A.

She had her nails done in a similar pattern but without the poison by her manicurist for Bree's Christmas Eve gathering. It wouldn't be a big party, not like the company party, merely a gathering of family and the neighbors who wanted to come by. Finger foods all around along with alcohol.

Bree's husband loved tasting bourbon. So did one of their neighbors. That meant bourbon tastings. Bree and Patten drank margaritas instead. The kids had sodas and passed around the finger foods, all with plenty of salt to sop up the alcohol.

Patten was on her third margarita, after all, she was essentially home and was most definitely not working, when the doorbell rang. It was late so she wasn't certain who would be turning up at the party.

She opened the door.

Mick Dawson stood there, clearly dressed for work.

"Merry Christmas," he said not smiling.

Patten raised an eyebrow.

He handed her her passport.

"You got away with it again," he said quietly. The music from behind her kept anyone else from hearing him, even if they were sober enough to understand.

"I don't know what you mean," Patten said quietly, keeping the little cat smile off her face.

"You know exactly. I don't know how you did it, but you did. There was the faintest bit of poison on your nails but the trace was so faint and wasn't

actually on the nail but in the bag with it that it could have been floating around the area and got on there so the DA doesn't want to charge you," Dawson said. "But I know."

"You think you know," Patten corrected him.

"I'll be watching you," Dawson said. He turned to leave.

Patten closed the door. She hoped he didn't have friends in Boston. For certain, she'd be particularly careful in L.A. and surroundings. In fact, she'd avoid working in that part of the country for a few years. Maybe she'd scale back her Bahamas trip and make sure the money from the Boston job lasted a bit longer so she could be pickier.

"What was that?" Bree asked.

Patten waved at her. "Nothing. I got my passport back in time for Christmas."

Bree gave her a big smile and a hug. "Best Christmas ever."

"Best indeed," Patten echoed.

An Unexpectedly Nice Christmas

The last tale is back to a cozier sort of mystery. It's not so cozy as A Craft Affair, nor is the main character a villain like many of the others. She's just a poor acupuncturist who is stuck at work on Christmas Eve. Her boss, however, is less than kind. When I was writing this tale, I had just read a story about a Santa Claus race and the idea of a bunch of people gathering all dressed as Santa intrigued me. These Santas aren't racing anywhere, they're just at a fictional bar somewhere in Pikeville. And while Pikeville, Kentucky is a real place, the bar and the acupuncture clinic are just figments of my imagination.

The falling snow had looked beautiful, despite the hardships it was causing, particularly for Jordan. But, Pikeville was like that. Both beautiful and hard. Jordan

had lived there almost six months and she could still be startled by the dichotomy.

For instance, when she'd come there from her Oregon home, to interview for a position as an acupuncturist, she'd thought the Appalachians were gorgeous. Winding her way through the mountain roads, less skittish than many, having lived in the Pacific Northwest where mountains were part of life, she'd loved the long curving slopes of the ancient range and the broad variety of trees, both evergreen and deciduous.

Cicadas had greeted her in the afternoons, their musical symphony relaxing. The smells had the slightly damp aroma of the mountains but were tinged with something else—something that reminded her of old dressers and rotten wood.

Getting into Pikeville, she'd been prepared to be enamored of the little town with its brick structures, but the roads were narrow and the buildings tall. Between that and the surrounding mountains, she'd felt claustrophobic. That, along with several crumbling brick facades, had made the town seem more threatening than welcoming.

Jordan had been prepared not to fit in. Not only was she an acupuncturist, she came from the left coast and subscribed to all sorts of liberal views. Still, with a burden of debt that would have made Atlas blanch, she couldn't pass up the money. And she'd been surprised by Pikeville again in the fall when there had been a pride festival in the park not far from the university.

Another plus to the town was the cost of living. Jordan had moved to an apartment slightly outside of town, a commute that wound through a gorgeous view of the ever-changing landscape. The greens of late summer followed by the rainbow hues of fall made her smile. Even the stark emptiness of winter, leaves having fallen, had an unexpected beauty.

If only Zach had been half the boss he'd presented himself to be. Two patients an hour four days a week, he'd told her. He saw that many and knew she would, too. Except that when Jordan came on, Zach had slowly stopped working so far as she could tell.

She'd worried his patients wouldn't like her, but Mrs. Caldwell had confided that she preferred Jordan because Zach had always had a wild streak when he was a boy, trying to get away with whatever he could. She would have waxed on about his high school exploits but Jordan had finished inserting needles and suggested her patient rest.

Mrs. Caldwell hadn't been the only one, just the most talkative and most explicit. Zach did have some people who insisted upon seeing him and he'd come in for a few hours on Thursday, the day Jordan was there to write up the newsletter and set their social media posts for the week. She was well paid for that part of her job, too, but it made her feel odd that she was doing that sort of marketing work for the clinic. She wondered how Zach survived before he'd hired her.

It wasn't until a few days ago that Jordan had come to realize what a slave driver Zach was. Just a little under a week before Christmas Eve, a tropical front had moved in sending rain down in the proverbial buckets saturating the ground which was followed by a cold front. With snow predicted for the eve of Christmas Eve, Jordan had asked for the day off.

"Why?" Zach had asked. He had his hipster vest on over a button-down flannel shirt and jeans rolled up in a narrow hem above his skinny ankles. The dark man bun was perfectly coifed as always.

"I'm not sure how good I'll be on the roads," Jordan said. "I'm not from around here and I live outside of town."

Zach waved her off. "You can't take off at every threat of snow. Just come in. We need the cash."

Jordan had tried to protest but Zach had given her a look, the look that said don't argue with him. She was reminded of a new patient, a young woman from the university, who had asked specifically for Jordan, because, she said she wanted to see a woman, not Zach.

Of course, because that was the way Jordan's life was going, the worst had happened. The saturated hills had let loose in what people were saying was a hundred-year-mud-slide event that closed the road that led to Jordan's apartment. To make things worse, the falling snow and the ice were making clearing it an even more major event than expected.

If the hotels hadn't been filled before, they were now, given that many motorists couldn't get through. There were other ways around the mountain, but those hillsides weren't in any better shape. Better stuck in Pikeville than buried beneath mud and slush.

Zach hadn't called to see if she had a place to stay and Jordan didn't call him. Instead, she figured she could walk across the street to the bar and get something to eat, maybe have some company, and then come back and sleep on one of the massage tables. She could use the smallest of the three treatment rooms and push the table up against the wall and curl on her side. Jordan didn't trust herself not to fall off while side sleeping on the narrowish massage tables. And a fall from that height onto wood floors would hurt.

The clinic was on the fourth floor of an office building that some days Jordan thought had been built new, fairly recently, and on others, she thought it had to be ancient. The elevator wheezed and chugged, moving as slowly as an eighty year old with advanced arthritis and asthma. The floors were narrow wood strips, the varnish worn in several places. The building itself seemed to lean over the street, hunching against the mountain behind it. Certainly, it was the tallest building in that area, and the brick façade was a brighter red than most.

The elevator smelled faintly of mothballs. The clinic smelled of moxa and herbs and sometimes the spice of Zach's too-heavy aftershave—but only when he bothered to come in.

Jordan had gone to the bar a few times with students she'd met. She was close to their age having gone to acupuncture school right after community college. The students made her feel more at home.

Inside the bar was modern and fairly bright with high, industrial-style ceilings. That evening, though, the students were a week gone home and the bar was having a drunken Santa contest.

The men drinking were all older and from the way they were hanging on the women in the bar, Jordan figured they'd all grown up without ever learning the meaning of the word consent. She had no desire to be fondled. Instead, she'd gotten an order of wings, which came with celery sticks, to go and ate in the tiny office of the clinic.

While the office was usually pleasant enough with sunlight streaming in through a window, that evening it was less than welcoming. Zach had gotten in a shipment of herbs, and several big boxes were scattered around the floor making the room feel not just small but cramped.

Christmas music from the bar drifted up as Jordan ate her lonely chicken wings and tried to remember if she'd ever felt lower. She couldn't afford to travel home for Christmas that year. She'd only just begun to make new friends and didn't really have anyone there. And her boss was a creep who had trapped her in the office for the holiday. Granted, the last wasn't something he meant to do, but his insistence that she work was the only reason she had gone into town.

After eating, Jordan tried to watch a movie on her laptop, but the boxes distracted her. While she had many office duties, opening inventory wasn't one of them. Zach was protective about the inventory. These boxes were from China. Jordan found it hard to believe he sold all the herbs he purchased from Asia. The herbs she sold came from the United States from reputable herbal manufacturers. Her teachers hadn't trusted the Chinese herbal formulas to be what they said they were.

Jordan itched to open the boxes up and put the bottles away, but she had a feeling Zach would be pissed. And she didn't want to have to deal with him if he were even a single bottle off. He'd probably make her pay retail prices for that single bottle even if it wasn't her fault.

Instead, Jordan retired to the little treatment room. She grabbed the three pillows from the small closet in the hall and the sheets and extra fleece blanket from beneath the sink that sat in the room. At least Zach had done that right and not relied on having to wash his hands in the bathroom sink down the hall. Once she'd made up the bed, Jordan curled on her side and tried to relax and drift off to the laughter and Christmas music just outside.

Just as she got to that place where she wasn't sure what was real and what was a dream, she heard something at the door. Zach had four different locks on the door, each requiring a different key. Jordan had turned off all the lights—she didn't want him angry with her for wasting energy. She hadn't even turned on the little space heater, though the overnight office temperature was lower than she'd like. She even had her jacket wrapped over her feet because they had a tendency to get chilled when she slept.

Jordan felt her heart rate spike as she sat, listening intently. It didn't sound like a break-in but the fact that no light came on to brighten the space beneath the door made the entry feel furtive. She waited, listening. She didn't move from the table, aware of the table's tendency to squeak just a bit when a patient climbed on or off, something that wouldn't be noticed over the other office sounds, but would stand out in the still night air.

Even the drunken Santas singing to the Christmas music across the street seemed quieter suddenly, as if they too, were holding their breath, waiting to see what happened up on the fourth floor of the office building. Jordan imagined them around the bar watching a large television tuned to a station showing a mysterious person breaking into the acupuncture clinic. For what, no one knew.

Jordan's reverie was broken by the sound of Zach's voice.

"Late shipment," Zach said. "I know I should have expected that this time of year..."

"Just get it sorted," a lower gruff voice said.

If Jordan had relaxed fractionally upon hearing Zach's voice, she tensed up at hearing this one. She didn't recognize it, but she recognized the tone. Villains in movies spoke with that tone of "don't mess with me." While Zach's voice had sent a chill tingle down her spine, this man sent Frosty the Snowman to give her a hug.

Fortunately, the door to the little exam room was closed and Jordan could think of no reason they'd come in there. Her jacket was wrapped around her feet, but she carefully unwrapped them in case she had to move. Her shoes, low boots, were on the floor, neatly beneath the table. She couldn't get to them unless she got off the table and doing so might make enough noise to attract their attention.

Jordan's purse was in the room, but she'd left the remains of her meal in the garbage in the office. Her heart thumped into her throat. Zach might figure out that she was staying there if he noticed.

From the other room, Jordan heard the sounds of someone cutting through cardboard. The heat clicked on with its usual wheeze and groan. It quieted too quickly for Jordan to take advantage of the sound to jump off the table. She could hope the Santas made noise. At least her phone was on Do Not Disturb for the evening.

Zach and the man he was with thumped and moved about the office next door. As the HVAC wound itself up to shut off, Jordan got ready to roll off the table. It made one final squeal and she rolled, landing lightly on the floor. She froze, waiting for any sign that Zach or the other man had noticed her movement. Nothing.

The room Jordan was in had cabinets around the sink, but no closet to hide in. Besides, the table wasn't normally against the wall, and moving it back to the center would make noise. Zach would know someone was there. A black metal fire escape, complete with rusted areas, ran down the side of the building from that window. While the windows did open easily, they made enough noise that Zach would hear her leaving.

If she was caught, Jordan could try and convince her boss she'd heard nothing and understood nothing, the latter completely true, though she had a few theories, all of them the sort of thing that made her want to run to the nearest police station. Given her overall luck that day, chances were the station would be short-staffed and no one would be around to help her.

More laughter, this time with a particularly raucous take on "I Saw Mommy Kissing Santa Claus" came from the bar. Jordan bit her lip. She carefully lowered herself until she was seated on the floor. The building tended to settle creating random squeaks now and then so she wasn't too worried Zach would make note of any sounds she might make.

First, her shoes. Jordan pulled those on. Her low boots had rubber soles because she'd worried about walking in the snow from her parking space to her apartment. Suddenly she was hit with homesickness for that little one-bedroom apartment. Alice McCreary lived next door with her three tuxedo cats, all of whom had quite an attitude. Alice loved to talk Jordan's ear off about those cats and their antics and Jordan, not having too much else to do, was happy enough to listen.

When Alice went off to visit her daughter for Thanksgiving, Jordan had cat sat for her. She would have been cat-sitting for Christmas, but Alice, unlike Zach had been cautious about the weather.

"I don't like that rain and then snow. You get a hunk of black ice and bam, you're done for. And I got my babies right here," Alice had said when she'd come over with a tin of homemade chocolate chip cookies for Jordan for Christmas. Jordan had planned to stop by the mall and pick something up for her neighbor, but that wasn't happening now.

It was too bad Zach wasn't a kinder boss. You'd think someone in healthcare would be more empathetic. Of course, Jordan had often wondered what he did to keep the clinic running given that he seemed less than enthusiastic about acupuncture. But she'd figured that maybe he was a good businessman. And if he could pay her well and let her do the parts of the work that she loved without worrying about income, she ought to be good with that.

But even before she sat trapped in the little room she'd known something was fishy. The set-up was just too good to be true. So now, here she was, hoping that neither man decided to wander down the hallway and look in the treatment rooms. Shoes on, along with her jacket, Jordan waited near the wall with the door, leaning against it only slightly.

She had her phone, but Zach would hear her talking on it. Some counties allowed texting to 911, but Jordan had never checked to see if Pikeville was in one of them. It wasn't like she planned to have to contact 911 and certainly not silently. She lived an ordinary life and ordinary people did not hide from potential criminals in their office.

"I gotta piss," the unfamiliar guy told Zach.

Jordan listened to him walk down the hallway. She held her breath, hoping he wouldn't look in the treatment room.

She waited, listening to the plumbing as the toilet flushed and the water splashed in the sink. He walked out, slowly. She heard him push the door open in the first treatment room. That door had been left open. The chill that had sent her shivering when the men entered overtook her now, but so did clarity.

Jordan swung her small purse across her body and hurried, as silently as possible to the window, which she raised. It rose more quietly than she'd thought it would, but not silent. She was out on the fire escape before the door behind her opened.

She didn't pause to look back but hurried down the stairs.

The laughter and singing from the drunken Santas was louder out there. The metal stairs were slick with the damp ice and snow and Jordan had to place her feet with more care than speed.

She felt the fire escape shake slightly as someone climbed out the window behind her. She wasn't anywhere near the ground. She had to keep moving.

Knowing she'd been caught, Jordan started yelling at the Santas. She wanted to wave an arm. The bar wasn't in direct line of sight to the building but she could see the parking area where some Santas, probably the losers, were outside walking off their drinks, designated drivers holding them up and letting them pace.

Jordan hurried as much as she could, taking the twisting switch-backs as fast as she thought she could do safely.

The man behind her went faster, his feet seeming surer, or else he was more desperate and less concerned about his welfare.

"FIRE!" Jordan screamed as loudly as she could. It got the attention of at least one of the designated drivers and she thought the person took out a phone.

As she turned to head down the final set of stairs, not sure how she was going to leap from there to the bottom, a hand grabbed at her arm. The stranger was close but he wasn't right behind her. He'd leaned forward. Jordan jerked her arm out of his grasp easily enough and he had to pause to get his balance again.

That allowed her to get to the drop ladder at the bottom of the fire escape. It took Jordan a couple of tries to get it to drop. By that time, the stranger was there, grabbing at her back, pulling her by her jacket towards him.

Feeling his hands pulling, Jordan screamed again, as loudly as she could.

This time, several of the designated drivers and their drunken Santas were looking over.

Jordan batted at the man, trying to remove his hands from her jacket. He held on.

She slipped out of her coat and lunged for the ladder, her feet barely hitting the rungs.

The stranger tossed her coat over the side and started to follow.

Jordan slipped off the steps and slid the last three rungs to the ground. She took off jogging over to the bar, shivering as a gust of wind hit her when she reached the street.

The stranger followed, moving faster than she did. He had to have some sort of ice traction on his shoes.

Jordan could barely stand upright. And it was a testament to the drunken Santas that they were standing in that parking lot at all.

She stepped out into the street, hoping to make it across the way.

A hand grabbed her shoulder.

Jordan screamed again.

This time the Santas in the parking lot all started jogging towards her.

She thought she heard "Hang on there, Rudolph!" but wasn't sure. She hoped that someone had called the police.

One of the Santas flopped down on the ground and struggled to get up. Another had better traction and flailed his way across the street.

The door to the bar had opened and a few people watched. After a moment of figuring out what had happened, several other people ran out of the bar.

One woman, dressed in an elf costume, had a canister of something, perhaps pepper spray, and sprinted across the street. Halfway across she threw her hands up and she slid towards the edge.

Jordan was having a hard time getting traction but her hands managed to grab the downspout on the edge of the building. Though she was certain she'd never have feeling in them again, holding on to the cold metal, she was able to slow her attacker down.

Snow flurries landed on her eyelashes and melted only slowly, making the world around her look even more surreal than it felt.

Then someone grabbed her by the front.

Another person pushed the stranger back.

The woman with the spray canister was screaming and spraying.

The Christmas carols from across the street disappeared beneath the whirring sirens of the police.

Jordan shivered as she was pulled into a bear hug by the group of Santas and their drivers. The elf woman stood over the stranger, her canister pointed at him.

The police got out of the cruiser to take custody of the man and to take statements. She was led to a police car where she could sit and warm up while she told her story to a man with a badge that said Officer Bennett. She didn't envy the other officer who was outside with the group from the bar.

The elf woman slipped into the backseat of the cruiser with her.

"Get out Mandy," Officer Bennett said quietly. He was turned in his seat, taking Jordan's statement. They'd only gotten to why Jordan was spending the night in the office.

"Hey. Police can be brutal. I'm just here to make sure you treat her fairly and all," Mandy the elf woman said.

Officer Bennett rolled his eyes.

"You know us," he said. It was almost a whine. Like he was hurt.

"How often do I get to make sure someone stays safe?" Mandy asked. "I read stuff on Facebook, you know."

Jordan wanted to laugh. Mandy's heart might be in the right place, but Jordan's hair and skin were fair enough that she wasn't exactly in the demographic for police brutality. Mandy patted her thigh.

"You can talk to him now, honey. I'm your witness." Mandy didn't slur her words so perhaps she'd not been a female Santa, but a judge.

Jordan told her story and mentioned Zach. When she got to his name, Mandy and Officer Bennett exchanged a significant look. Then Bennett smiled.

He winked at Mandy and got out of the car.

"What was that about?" Jordan asked, suddenly fearful that she'd stumbled into a ring of some sort that included the police.

"Don't you worry, honey," Mandy said again, patting her thigh. "Benny's been hoping for a promotion for months now. Catching Zach Ferguson will probably do it for him."

"What do you mean?" Jordan asked.

"You worked for Zach and you really don't know?" Mandy asked.

"I didn't," Jordan said. "I mean I knew it seemed weird where he got his money but I thought maybe family…"

Mandy started laughing as Jordan said family.

"No one around here has the kind of money Zach has," Mandy said. "And his parents are the epitome of poor white trash. Zach was always smart and everyone knew if they needed an answer they went to him. No surprise he figured out how to smuggle drugs. Everyone knew he was distributing, but there was no proof. Not even enough to get a judge to get a warrant, but you gave the police that."

Jordan nodded.

"It's going to be a great holiday for some folks who've wanted to see him taken down," Mandy said. "But not so great for you, huh? 'Cause that office is going to be a crime scene and I doubt there's room in the hotels."

And just like that Jordan was feeling far less comfortable.

Mandy pulled out her phone and started texting. "I live in a dump and already have my cousin crashing on the sofa for the holiday so I can't take you. I mean I will if no one else can, but it'll be cramped and you'll be on the floor. I know someone in campus housing. Maybe they got an empty room they can let you use for a few. You did do a huge favor. And believe me, the campus was a main area that Zach's dealers were selling to."

"Are you sure he had drugs?" Jordan asked. No one had come out of the building.

"I'm sure," Mandy said. "It's like the worst kept secret."

Jordan had thought that. It seemed logical. "What comes from China?"

"Fentanyl," Mandy said. "Derrick, the big fat Santa that's bent over across the street, vomiting, is a detective. He's off tonight, of course, but I bet he's sobering up quick. He has a theory that Zach only studied acupuncture to give him a legit excuse to travel overseas and make connections. Not like he was a very good acupuncturist. Several folks you've treated are already better and they got nothing from Zach. A few buy drugs from him, but they ain't talking."

"You sure know a lot," Jordan said, looking at Mandy.

"I work at the diner near the highway," Mandy said. "I hear everything. And I've lived here all my life so I know everyone." She winked at Jordan.

They sat in silence watching the snowfall.

Mandy's phone dinged twice. "Rog didn't have anything in student housing, but he contacted Diana. They had a late cancellation on a room just come through so there's a place at the Schneider Hotel across from the park."

"Isn't it expensive?" Jordan asked.

"On the house," Mandy said. "Considering the favor you did for the town, you probably won't have to pay for meals or hotels or anything in the town proper for months."

Jordan shrugged. "I was just trying to save my life. Although, if Zach goes to jail, I'll be out of a job."

"We'll work it out," Mandy assured her. "Probably something so that you can keep working as an acupuncturist. Maybe you can buy him out of the practice. He'll need the money. Zach spends it like it's water or something. And I hear trials aren't cheap."

Jordan smiled. The bar was still playing Christmas carols and just as Officer Bennett and a man in plain clothing that walked with the confident walk of a police officer came out of the building with Zach in handcuffs, the carol changed to We Wish You a Merry Christmas.

A couple of the Santas who had been milling around knocked on the door of the cruiser and held up Jordan's coat, which, unfortunately, looked pretty wet.

Mandy opened the door.

"Come on over to the bar. It's warm and we'll get this dried out for you!" One of the Santa's called. He didn't seem all that drunk.

Jordan let them lead her, along with Mandy, across the street. A few whoops and whistles went up from around the bar, all of them from Santas who looked a bit too out of it to stand up.

"So what's up with a drunken Santa contest?" Jordan asked Mandy as they were seated at a table.

"Well, it's like this..." Mandy said, starting her tale, a wicked grin across her face.

Jordan listened intently as her new friend talked and realized as she drank an orange juice brought over by a tottering Santa that she half-expected to try and cop a feel, that Pikeville had once again managed to surprise her. In fact, by the time she left the bar it was Christmas Eve Day, and not a single Santa had tried to feel her up or made a lewd comment. In fact, most of them had called home to find out if their wives and girlfriends had any extra clothing Jordan could borrow.

Christmas wasn't going to be so bad after all.

About Bonnie Elizabeth

Bonnie Elizabeth has been writing since she was eight years old when she wrote her first book on several pieces of lined paper. The manuscript has long since been lost.

Since that time she has worked at a variety of jobs including veterinary receptionist, cemetery administrator and licensed acupuncturist. She has continued to write in a variety of venues, from blogging to writing about acupuncture under her full name and title, Bonnie Koenig, LAc.

Bonnie writes the popular Whisper series of novels as well as writing a variety of short fiction. You can find her books and stories at all your favorite ebook retailers.

Stay in Touch